A Journey in the Moon Balloon

When Images Speak Louder Than Words

Written and Illustrated by
Joan Drescher

Jessica Kingsley *Publishers*
London and Philadelphia

DISCLAIMER
Names and identity of the persons whose stories are told in this book have been changed.
Some individuals described in this book are composites of several different patients, used to make a point or to tell their story.
These stories, though factual, are told not for reporting purposes but in order to illustrate a point of the author.

First edition published in 1996 by the Association for the Care of Children in Hospitals.
Second edition published in 2005 by The Moon Balloon Project, Inc.

This expanded edition published in 2015 by
Jessica Kingsley Publishers
73 Collier Street
London N1 9BE, UK
and
400 Market Street, Suite 400
Philadelphia, PA 19106, USA

www.jkp.com

Book Design by Susan Bayley

Copyright © Joan Drescher 1996, 2005, 2015
Foreword copyright © Joan Borysenko 2015

THE MOON BALLOON ® and The Moon Balloon design are trademarks registered in the
United States Patent and Trademark Office, Nos. 4022621, 4028393, and 4026191.

All rights reserved. No part of this publication may be reproduced in any material form (including photocopying or storing it in any medium by electronic means and whether or not transiently or incidentally to some other use of this publication) without the written permission of the copyright owner except in accordance with the provisions of the Copyright, Designs and Patents Act 1988 or under the terms of a licence issued by the Copyright Licensing Agency Ltd, Saffron House, 6-10 Kirby Street, London EC1N 8TS. Applications for the copyright owner's written permission to reproduce any part of this publication should be addressed to the publisher.

Warning: The doing of an unauthorised act in relation to a copyright work may result in both a civil claim for damages and criminal prosecution.

Library of Congress Cataloging in Publication Data
A CIP catalog record for this book is available from the Library of Congress

British Library Cataloguing in Publication Data
A CIP catalogue record for this book is available from the British Library

ISBN 978 1 84905 730 1
eISBN 978 1 78450 100 6

Printed and bound in China

Contents

Foreword by Joan Borysenko

Introduction: "The Power of Art to Help Heal" by Vivien Marcow-Speiser

Part I:
The Moon Balloon — 7
    A Note to Kids — 8

Part II:
When Images Speak Louder Than Words — 38
    Your Companion for Inspiration — 39
    Stories from the Kart: Inspiration on Wheels — 40
    The Magician: *Transformation* — 42
    Queen Aileen: *Courage* — 44
    Uncovering Light Under Darkness: *Hope* — 45
    The Pain-Free Hat: *Freedom of Spirit* — 46
    "Bonbolita": *Transforming Stress Through Beauty* — 48
    The Blue Box: *Gratitude* — 49
    You've Got Mail: *Unconditional Love* — 50
    Martin's Mandalas: *Beauty and Joy* — 52
    Rejection: *Finding Self Love* — 53
    Dreamsweeper: *When Images Transform* — 54

Part III:
Sharing Art Activities — 56
    Being Present for a Child — 57
    "Making Inspiration Soup" — 60
    You Can Do It — 61
    Mandalas: Cathedral Windows — 62
    Cardboard Mandalas — 62
    Scratchboard Art — 63
    The Pain-Free Hat — 63
    The Mailbox — 64
    A Treasure Box — 64
    The Magic Wand — 65
    Crown — 65
    Free Drawing Murals — 66
    Butterfly Bouquet — 66
    The Moon Balloon: Simple Drawing Techniques — 67
    Supply List — 67

Part IV:
Outreach and Resources:
Art and Healing Around the World — 68

Acknowledgements — 71
About Joan Drescher — 72

Foreword

by Joan Borysenko, Ph.D.

It is somewhere in the mid-1980s. I am walking through the corridors of Boston Children's Hospital, looking for the office of a research colleague. I take a wrong turn in the oncology unit and find myself in a treatment room. In the center, lying face up on a gurney, is a little boy of about five receiving a transfusion. His eyes are closed and he is absolutely still, as white as the sheet on which he is lying. I close the door softly, so as not to disturb the child, and continue on my way. But the ghostly image haunts me. I have two young boys of my own. It's bad enough for a child to be ill, I think, but the barren feeling of that lonely room has me in tears.

When I mention the incident to my colleague she tells me about a mural at the Joint Center for Radiation Therapy at Brigham and Women's Hospital / Children's Hospital that brings color, life, and hope to the patients. Rather than lying alone on the radiation table and staring up at a white ceiling and glaring lights, the kids see a life-size figure painted in one corner, holding a bunch of kite strings. The colorful kites fan out around the top of the room, each containing a healing symbol from a different culture. The conscious mind is delighted by the imagery, while the unconscious mind absorbs the message of hope and healing that the kites convey.

Who is the artist, I wonder, who transformed a sterile radiation room into a nurturing healing environment? I am told that her name is Joan Drescher. I note it for future reference, and return to my office at Boston's Beth Israel Hospital, where I am Associate Director, Division of Behavioral Medicine. There we study the effects of mind on body; how stress drains the life force and predisposes to disease; and how hope and compassion engender health and support healing.

At that time, the field of arts and healing was in its infancy. Joan Drescher was at the leading edge of a nascent revolution in hospital design. A seminal study published in 1984 in the prestigious journal *Science*, by psychologist Roger Ulrich, was among the first to validate scientifically the healing power of natural beauty. Surgical patients with bedside windows looking out on green trees healed more quickly, required less pain medication, and had fewer postsurgical complications than patients whose rooms faced a brick wall.

Soon after hearing about Joan's healing mural I bumped into her at a meditation center on the South Shore of Boston where, it turns out, we both lived. In a short time we became fast friends and created a women's circle together.
Two books came out of that circle. The first, *On Wings of Light*, is about how we humans begin our life as magical children and gradually lose touch with the awe and wonder of our younger years, and how we can recover a childlike sense of connection with the beauty and wholeness of life. It was a collaboration: I wrote the text, and Joan D. created

the illustrations. It was a magical process, filled with synchronicity. I would change the text and call Joan to tell her about it, only to find that she'd already changed the illustration to reflect my change!

The second book that came out of the women's circle was Joan's *Moon Balloon*. Children who are ill or traumatized, she reasoned, often have no words to express their feelings. Even if they do, it can be hard to give them voice. Worse still, the words may fail to be received and witnessed in a loving way. She felt strongly guided to create a book - a journey in a series of hot air balloons representing a spectrum of emotions - that offers a safe and natural way for children to express their feelings and share them with others.

As a cell biologist and psychologist I have studied the mechanisms through which emotions link mind and body. The bottom line is that unexpressed feelings are a common - sometimes immensely powerful - source of stress and immune suppression.

And the opposite is also true. Fear expressed can be a doorway to hope, connection, and health. Anger given a voice can lead to forgiveness, resolution, or necessary change. Sadness can bring two hearts together and open the door to unexpected grace. The research study that came out of Joan's work with *The Moon Balloon* demonstrated that the expression of feelings significantly improved the quality of life for both hospitalized children and their parents.

In this precious new book, *When Images Speak Louder Than Words*, Joan tells the stories of children with whom she has worked, using *The Moon Balloon*. Each story is one of deep humanity that will touch you to the core. I was particularly moved by the story, "You've Got Mail." What a brilliant idea Joan had, to put mailboxes on her Imagination Kart so that kids and caregivers could create personalized mailboxes, then send each other letters verbalizing things that might be too difficult to say out loud. Letters that can be saved and cherished. Letters whose love can keep on giving for a lifetime. I'm going to use mailbox-making as an activity with my grandchildren.

Joan's instructions for how to use *The Moon Balloon* and art in general go beyond working with ill or traumatized children. The ideas described so clearly and compassionately in this new book are useful for all children, including the child who still lives in the heart of every adult. This book is a classic in the field of art and healing, a true work of the soul by a humble, caring woman who has transformed the lives of thousands.

Joan Borysenko is a distinguished pioneer in integrative medicine. A world-renowned expert in the mind/body connection, her work has been foundational in an international health-care revolution that recognizes spirituality and integrative medicine as an essential part of health and healing. She holds a doctorate in medical sciences from Harvard Medical School and is a licensed psychologist and the author of the New York Times best seller, *Minding the Body, Mending the Mind*, as well as numerous other books, including *Your Soul's Compass; What is Spiritual Guidance?*, and *On Wings of Light*, which she co-authored with Joan Drescher.

Dedication

I give special thanks to my husband, Ken, who has always supported my work, every step along the way.
I also dedicate this book to the young patients suffering with chronic illness and their families, and the doctors, nurses, social workers, child life specialists and many caregivers - heroes who walk the journey together with them.

Introduction: The Power of Art to Help Heal

This book is a miracle of hope, love, caring and commitment.

It is a testament to the power of the arts in healing and to the compassionate care and life-affirming work that Joan Drescher engages in as a daily practice.

The book bears witness and speaks eloquently for itself in the words and images generated in this dialog between Joan and her patients. Moving between written and visual images, and the unwritten and unseen worlds in its power, it illuminates and affirms life in even the darkest of moments.

Joan offers children, caregivers, parents and others practical hands-on tools for engaging in the arts' curative powers. With its many concrete examples and clearly articulated tools, this deeply engaging book includes clear instructions and guidelines for using art as a way to have difficult conversations and elicit life-enhancing responses to troubled times.

This gem of a book offers artists and non-artists alike viable and easily accessible methods to reach children and adults in vulnerable moments and circumstances, and to reach deep within to access images of healing, hope and inspiration.

Vivien Marcow-Speiser

Vivien Marcow-Speiser, Ph.D., BC-DMT, LMHC, NCC, REAT is a Professor and the Director of National, International and Collaborative Programs in the Graduate School of Arts and Social Sciences at Lesley University. Her work has allowed her unparalleled access to groups across the United States, Israel and internationally. She has used the arts as a way of communicating across borders and cultures and believes in their power to create the conditions for personal and social change and transformation.

Part 1

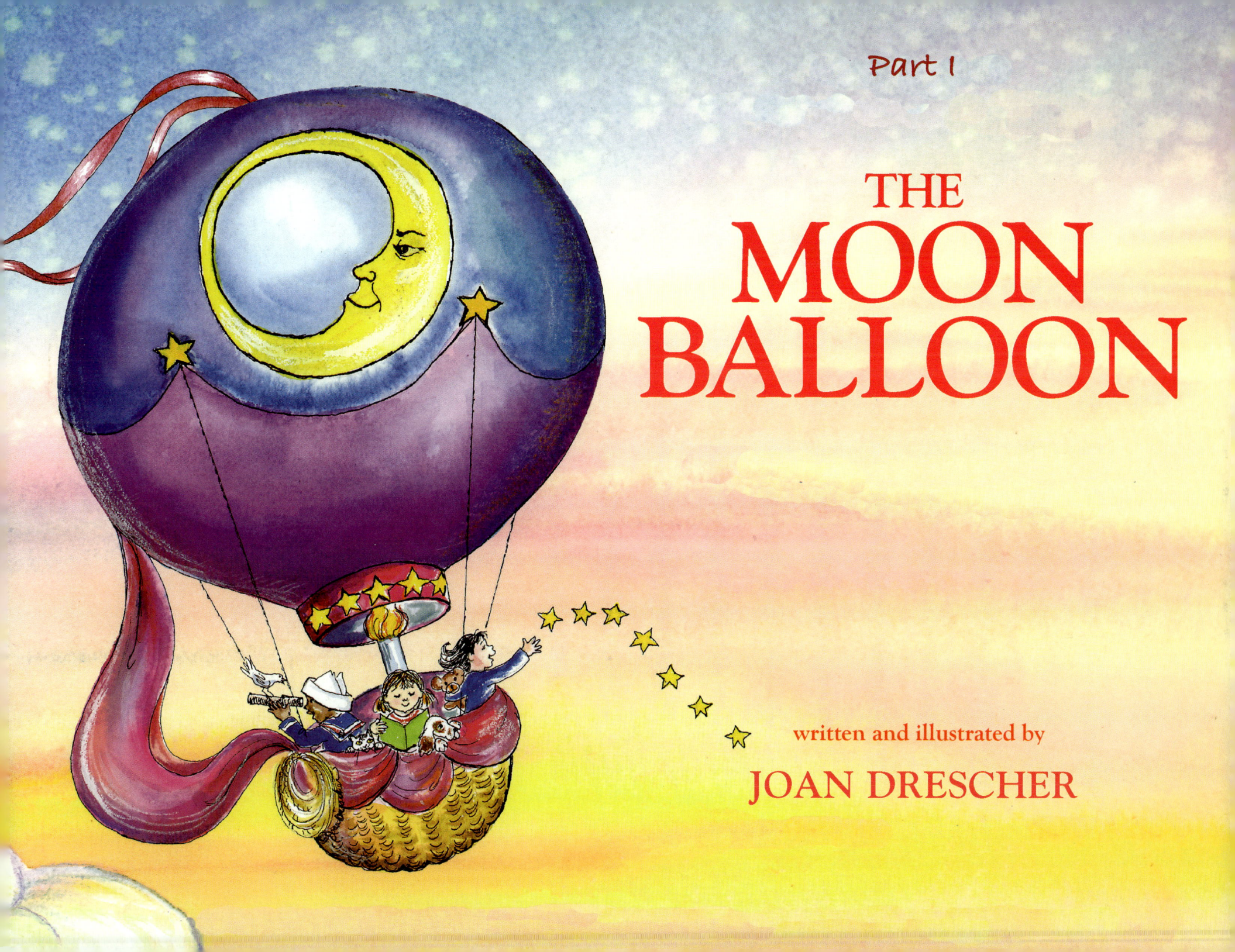

THE MOON BALLOON

written and illustrated by
JOAN DRESCHER

A NOTE TO KIDS

The Balloon is a special book for you to use and enjoy. It will take you on a trip in an air balloon! During your trip you will get in touch with the most powerful gift you have, your own imagination.

When you're unhappy you often forget the joy in life. Maybe you have to stay in bed when you wish you were out playing with other kids!

IT'S NOT FAIR!

You might feel alone, sad, helpless, happy and angry all at the same time. These feelings are o.k. It is natural to feel them.

Using your imagination The Balloon will take you to the Field of Balloons where each balloon you visit is a feeling you might have. Have fun with them by writing and drawing your feelings on each balloon.

It is [o.k.] to make extra 🌞 photocopies of the black and white pages, so you can write in it again and again. Sharing the book with others can be wonderful, 💕 but if you want to keep it private 🗝 that's [o.k.,] too. This is your book.

Have fun!

I hope The 🌙 Balloon will (comfort) you when you are feeling 😞 down, give you giggles 😁😁😁 as well as ⭐ courage ⭐ and help you get in touch with your own powerful magic… your imagination.

But most of all, I hope The 🌙 Balloon will become your friend.

♥♥ Love ♥♥

Joan Drescher

The Moon Balloon
is waiting to take you
on a journey
to your favorite place.

So climb in the basket.
You may bring a friend
or a pet.

In the bottom of the basket
you will find a slip of paper
with flight instructions.

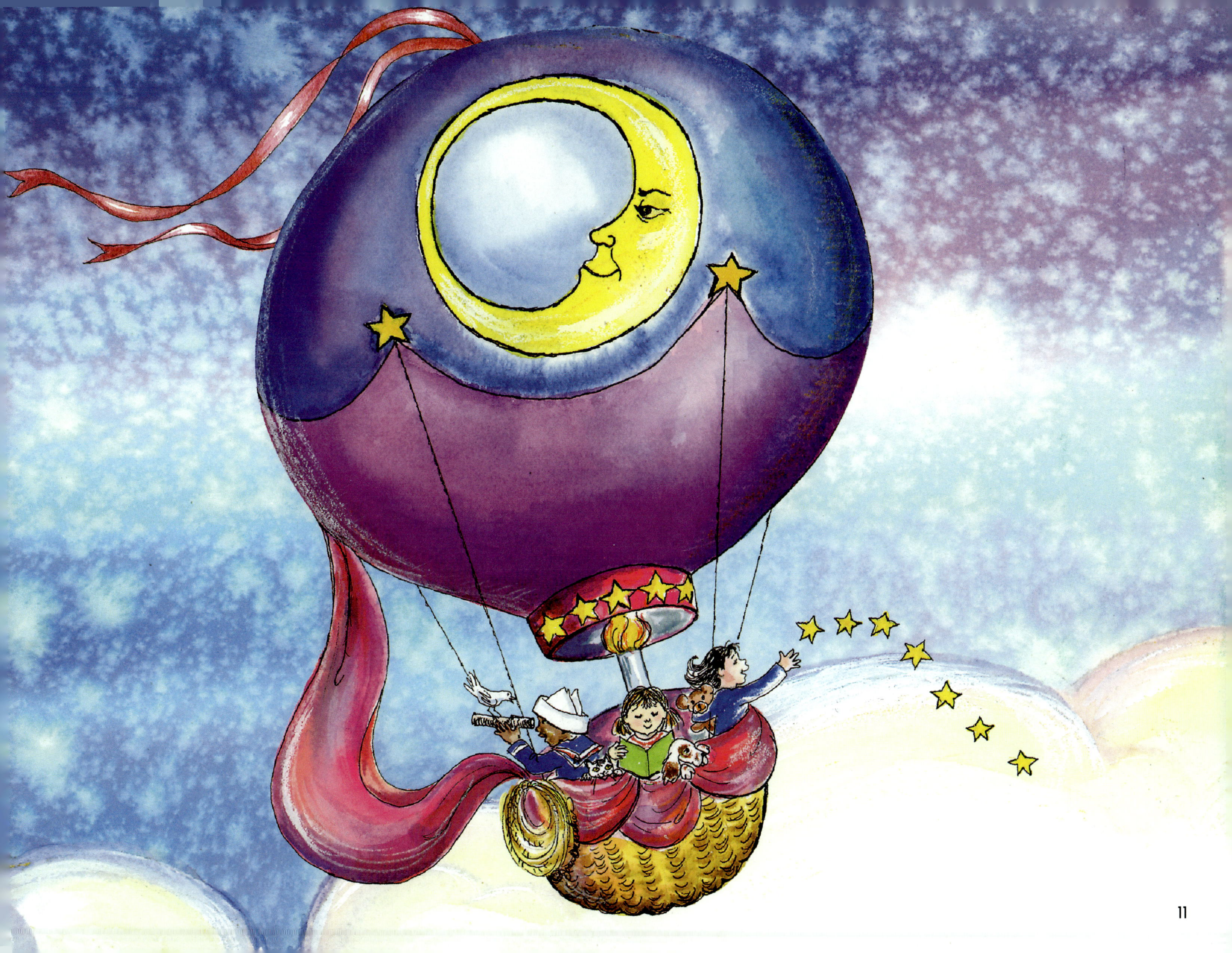

FEAR

ANXIOUS FEELINGS

WORRY

INSTRUCTIONS FOR TAKE OFF

1. Take a deep breath and let it out.

2. Use the fire in the Air Balloon to spark your imagination.

3. Every balloon has a sandbag full of heavy things like fear, worry and anxiety.

4. In order to go up, you need to be light. So let go of the sandbags one by one.

5. Drop fear, worry and anxious feelings out with the sand.

6. When you are done you will feel very light and your balloon will begin to go up.

7. In the bottom of the basket are seven stars. As you begin to rise, send each star to someone you love.

You can name each star

THE FIELD OF BALLOONS

BUTTERFLY BALLOON
- Butterflies in your stomach
- Anxious feelings
- Throw out worry
- Fear

STAR BALLOON
- Courage is your own star
- Wish with the fish

ANGRY BALLOON
- A place to scream and yell and go to when things go wrong.
- Throw away Bad feelings
- Bad moods
- Things you can't stand

TEAR BALLOON
- Feeling Helpless
- Disappointed
- Hurt
- Sad
- It's ok to cry

During your flight you will see soft white clouds passing by you. The wind sings a song in your ears.

Soon you will come to a place in the sky where you see tiny bits of color. As you get closer you see it is the Field of Balloons.

SUN BALLOON
- Peace
- Beauty
- Summer days
- Warm feelings

PEACE BALLOON
- Resting quietly
- Sweet dreams
- Wind songs
- Feeling Safe
- Welcome

GIGGLE BALLOON
- Joy
- Laughter
- Giggles
- Smiles
- Fun
- Jokes
- Ha-Ha
- Ho-Ho
- Tee-Hee
- Fun

STRESS BALLOON
- Winning and losing
- Time running out
- Pollution
- Conflict
- Noise
- 2 Fast
- 2 Much
- 2 Many Things
- Beep, Ring, Boom!, Ring
- No time for me
- Bad TV news
- Too much
- Too fast
- Too loud
- Too many things to do

LOVE BALLOON
- Open your heart
- Give to others
- Be kind
- Miracles
- Wonder
- Hugs
- Magic
- Joy

Each balloon is a feeling you might have.
Sometimes we have more than one feeling. All of these feelings are o.k.

You can choose to visit whichever balloon you like, depending on how you feel. Visit them again and again whenever you like!

15

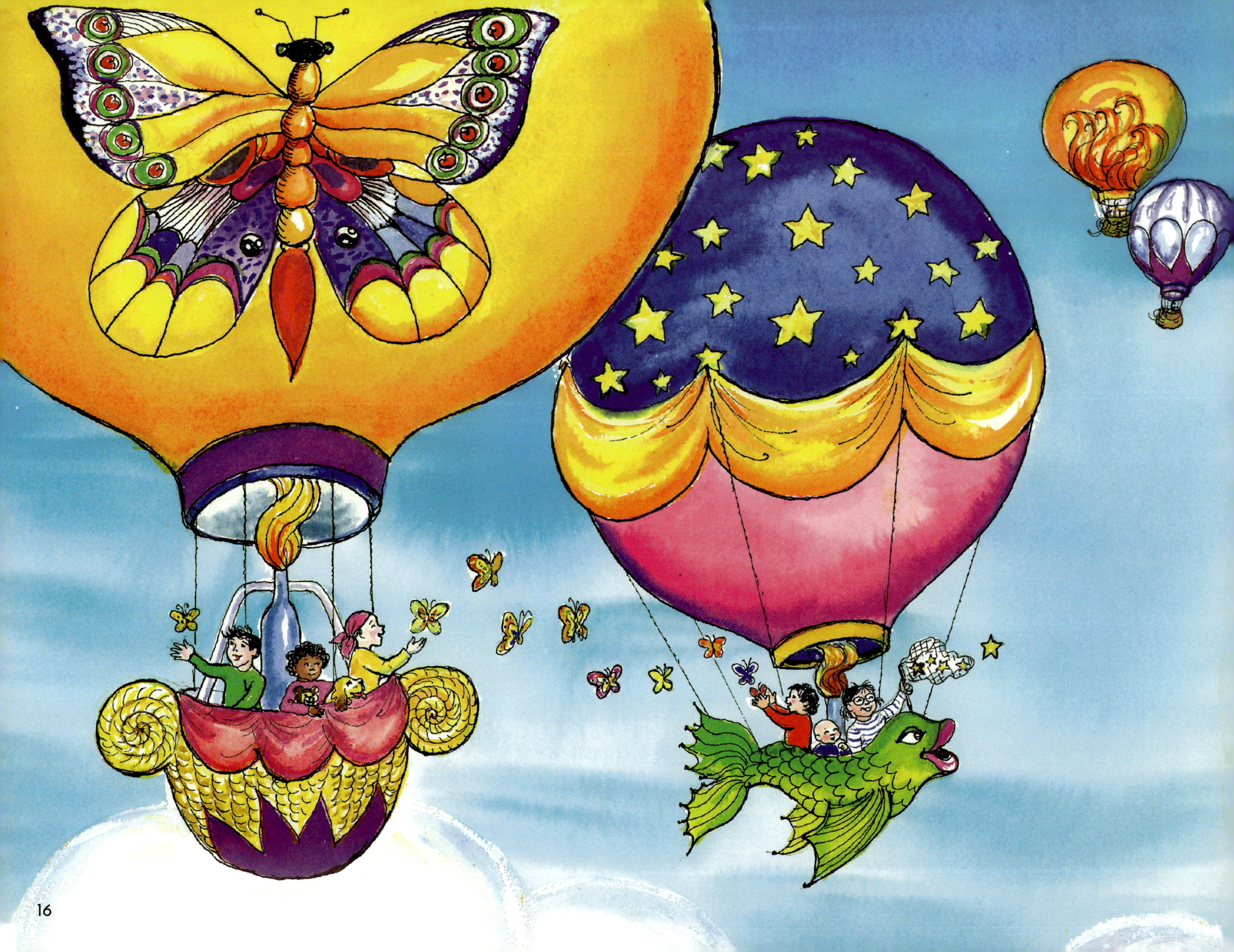

If you are feeling scared or have butterflies in your stomach, climb into the Butterfly Balloon and throw them out.
The Star Balloon will surely catch them.

The Star Balloon has a fish for a basket. Make a wish with the fish in the Star Balloon. He will give you a special star to give you courage.

Write your wish upon this star.

My magical star is always with me.
It is my own imagination.
It lights my way in darkness and gives me courage.

The Sun Balloon will warm you and comfort you. Its bright sunshine fills you with beauty and warmth. It will take you to the Land of Summer Days where you can hear birds singing, smell wild flowers and feel the warmth of the sun on your back.

⭐ I see the light of the sun.
I feel warmth.
I feel safe.

SUMMER TREASURES

Draw a picture of your favorite summer day.
Fill the basket with treasures you found on the beach,
in the grass or just anywhere.

The Stress Balloon is a place to go when everything seems like too much! You can leave a lot of things that are driving you crazy in this balloon.

⭐ Sometimes I feel so stressed that I'm ready to explode! Before I pop, I visit the Stress Balloon.

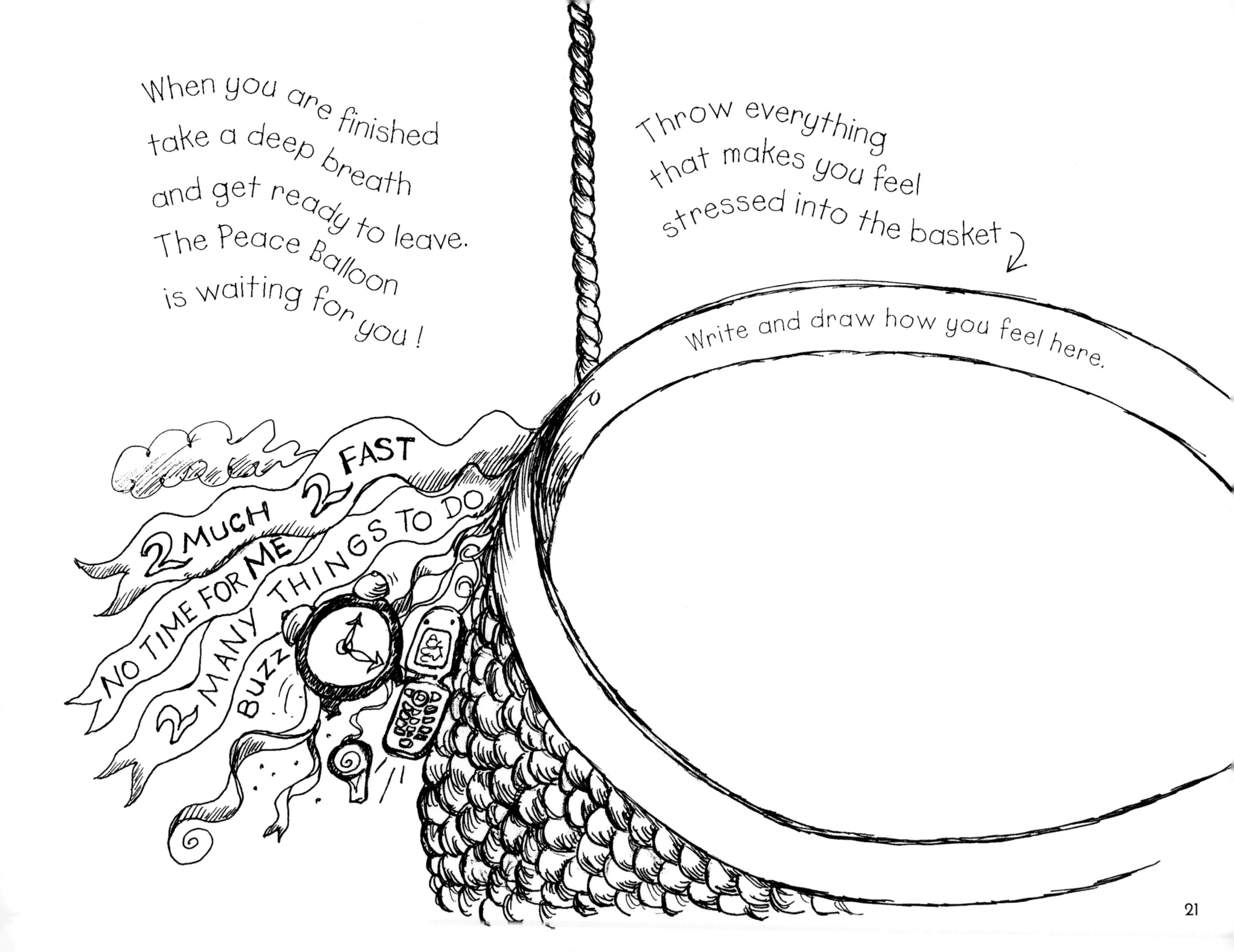

When you are finished take a deep breath and get ready to leave. The Peace Balloon is waiting for you!

Throw everything that makes you feel stressed into the basket

Write and draw how you feel here.

2 MUCH 2 FAST
NO TIME FOR ME
2 MANY THINGS TO DO
BUZZ

The Peace Balloon
is a safe quiet place.
The wind rocks you gently
and sings you a lullaby.
Your balloon rises slowly
into the clouds. Relax,
you don't have to do
anything here.
Just be yourself.

⭐ I rest quietly and visit the peaceful place inside of me.
I feel welcome and safe. I can visit this place whenever I like.

Close your eyes and take a deep breath.
Let your mind go to the peaceful place inside of you.

Put your favorite dreams in the basket.

Pick a cloud. Write down a dream. Remember your dreams are always here waiting for you!

The Tear Balloon
  is for catching your tears.
  It is all right to feel
  sad and cry when
  you're in the Tear Balloon.

Fill the basket full of pain,
  disappointment, sadness
  and hurtful feelings.

⭐ I give myself permission to feel my saddest feelings.
  It's o.k. for me to cry.

You can write or draw what makes you feel sad and put it in the empty basket of the Tear Balloon.

You can also draw yourself when you feel sad or alone, or just fill the basket with tears.

It is very deep!

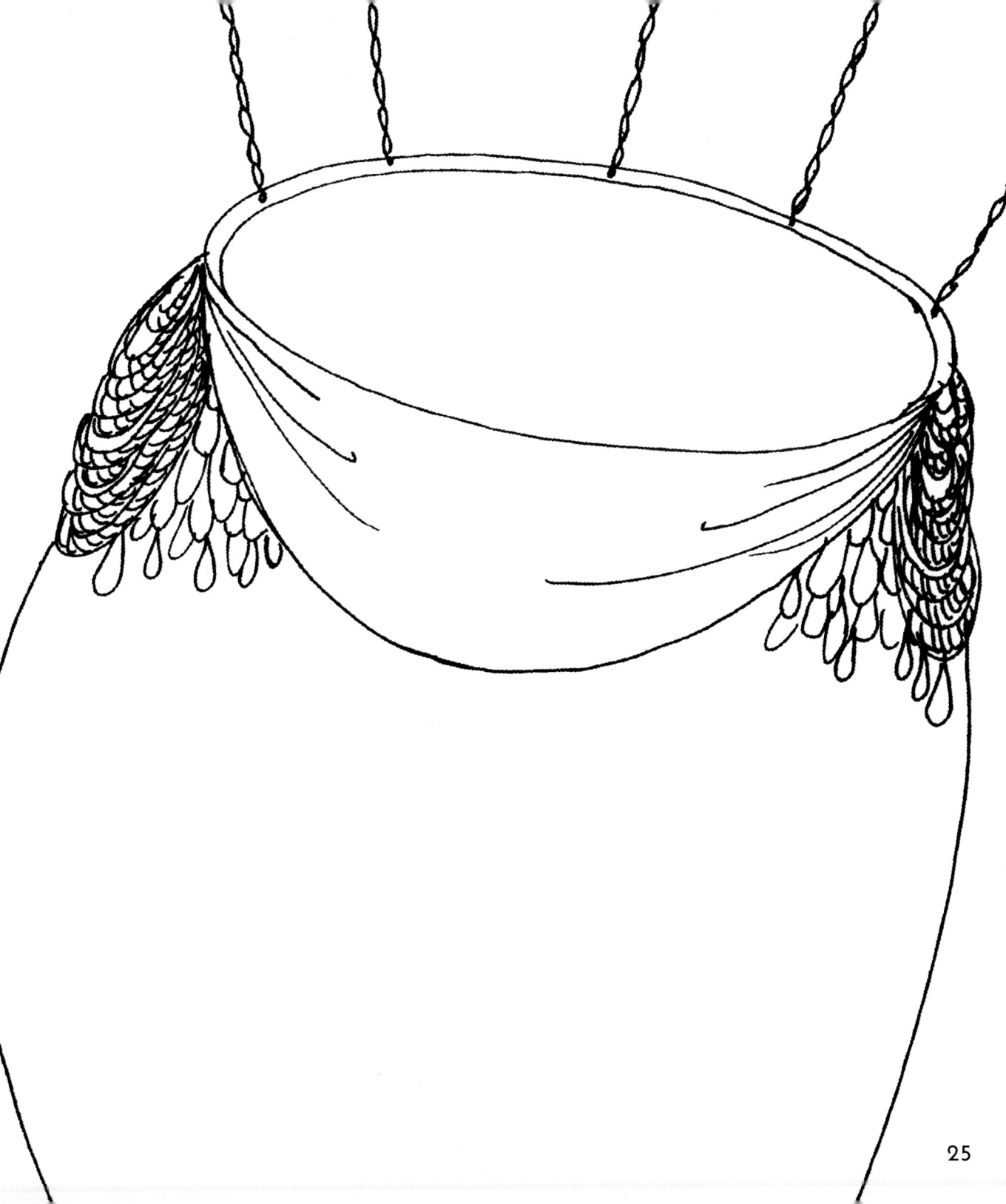

The Angry Balloon
is the place to go
when you're feeling
really mad or upset.
You can put all the
things that make you mad
in this balloon.
It is a place to let go
of bad feelings.

Sometimes
when things go wrong
we think it is our fault.

It is not your fault.

⭐ It is o.k. to be angry.

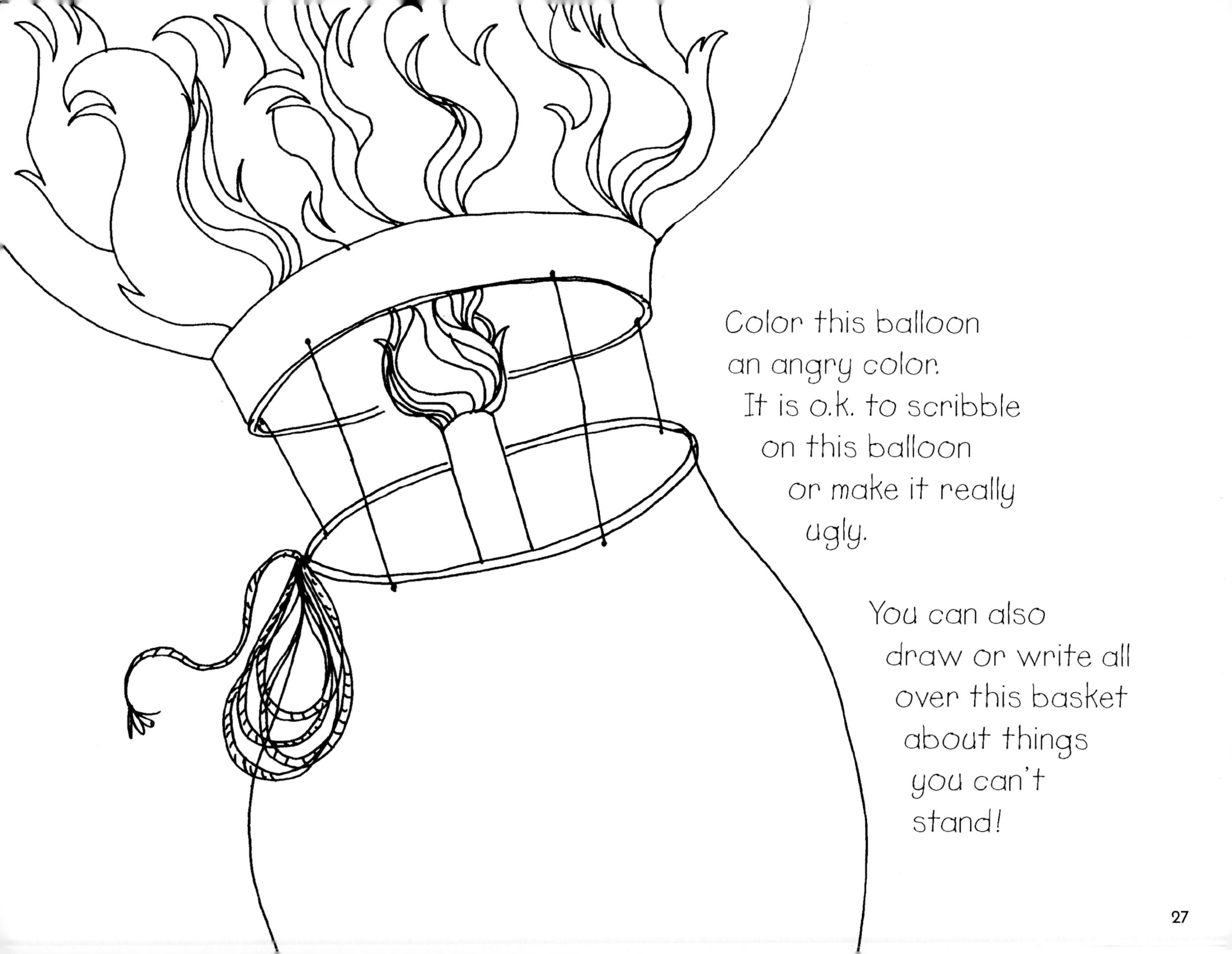

Color this balloon an angry color. It is o.k. to scribble on this balloon or make it really ugly.

You can also draw or write all over this basket about things you can't stand!

Tickle your toes
and make a funny face.

The Giggle Balloon
will take you to
the laughing place.

Close your eyes and turn
the corners of your mouth up
into a smile. Let the smile go into a giggle.

As you giggle your balloon goes higher
and higher up into the clouds, where
you laugh out loud with the birds in the sky!

Ha Ha Ha Ha

Ho Ho Ho

Giggle Tee-Hee

The more you laugh, the higher you go...

Now, throw a party in the sky.
Laughter is the only gift you need to bring.
But you must share it with others.

Knock!
Knock!
Who's there?

Fill in

Fill in

Fill in your favorite jokes and riddles!

Invite whomever you wish.

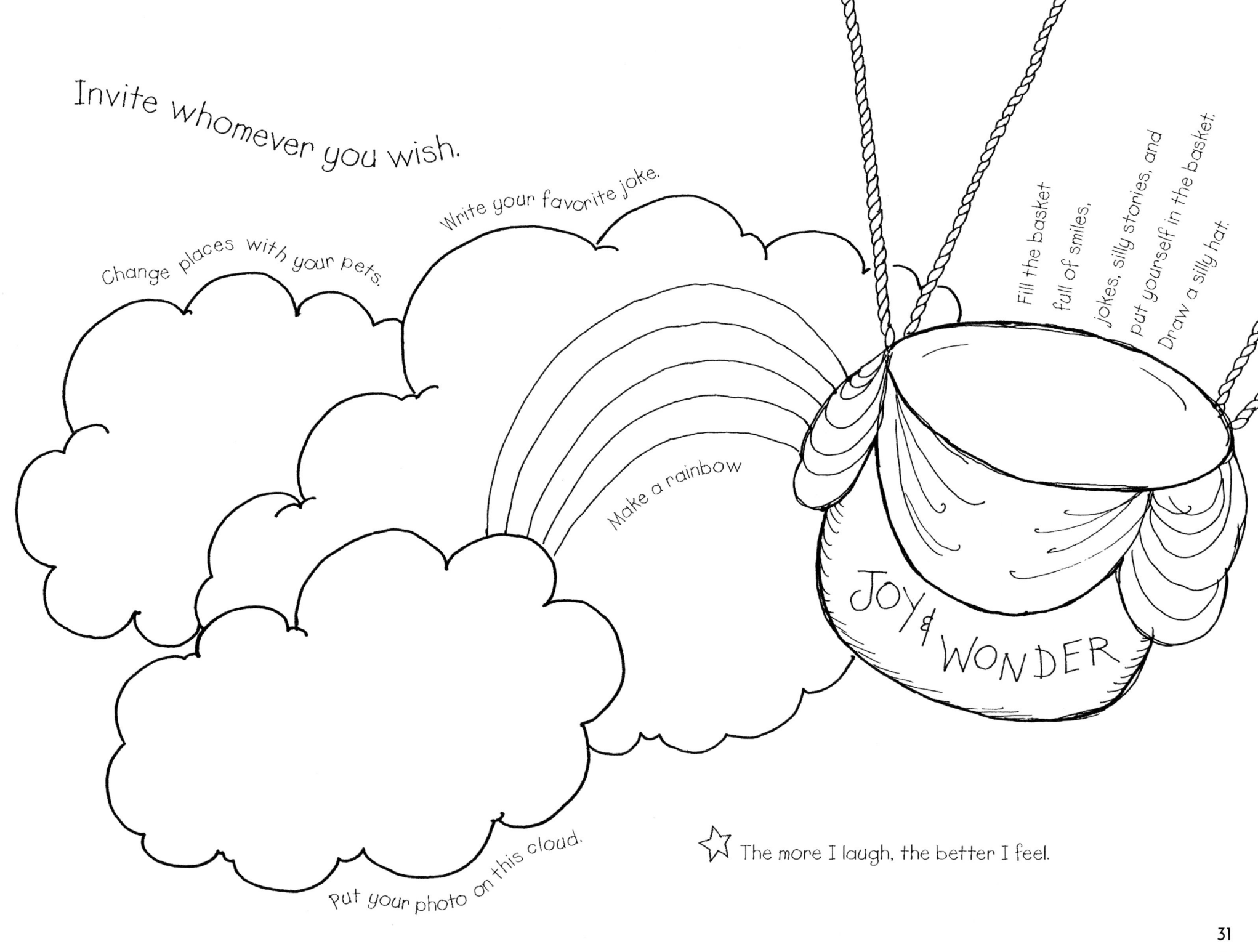

Change places with your pets.

Write your favorite joke.

Make a rainbow

Put your photo on this cloud.

Fill the basket full of smiles, jokes, silly stories, and put yourself in the basket. Draw a silly hat.

JOY & WONDER

☆ The more I laugh, the better I feel.

31

When you are
feeling alone and unloved,
climb into the Love Balloon.
This basket is filled with hearts.
Close your eyes and think of all the
people you could send love to.
If you need help, call on the messenger
birds that live on the nearby cloud,
Soon, the love you send out will
come back to you.
The Love Balloon is for miracles.

Write your name on a heart and send yourself love.

⭐ I am a beautiful, special person.
There is no one in the world like me.
I give myself a hug.

Write the names of people you want to send love to on the hearts.

You can visit
the Moon Balloon
anytime you like
and go anywhere you like.

Just close your eyes
and use your imagination.

It is the most powerful
magic you have.

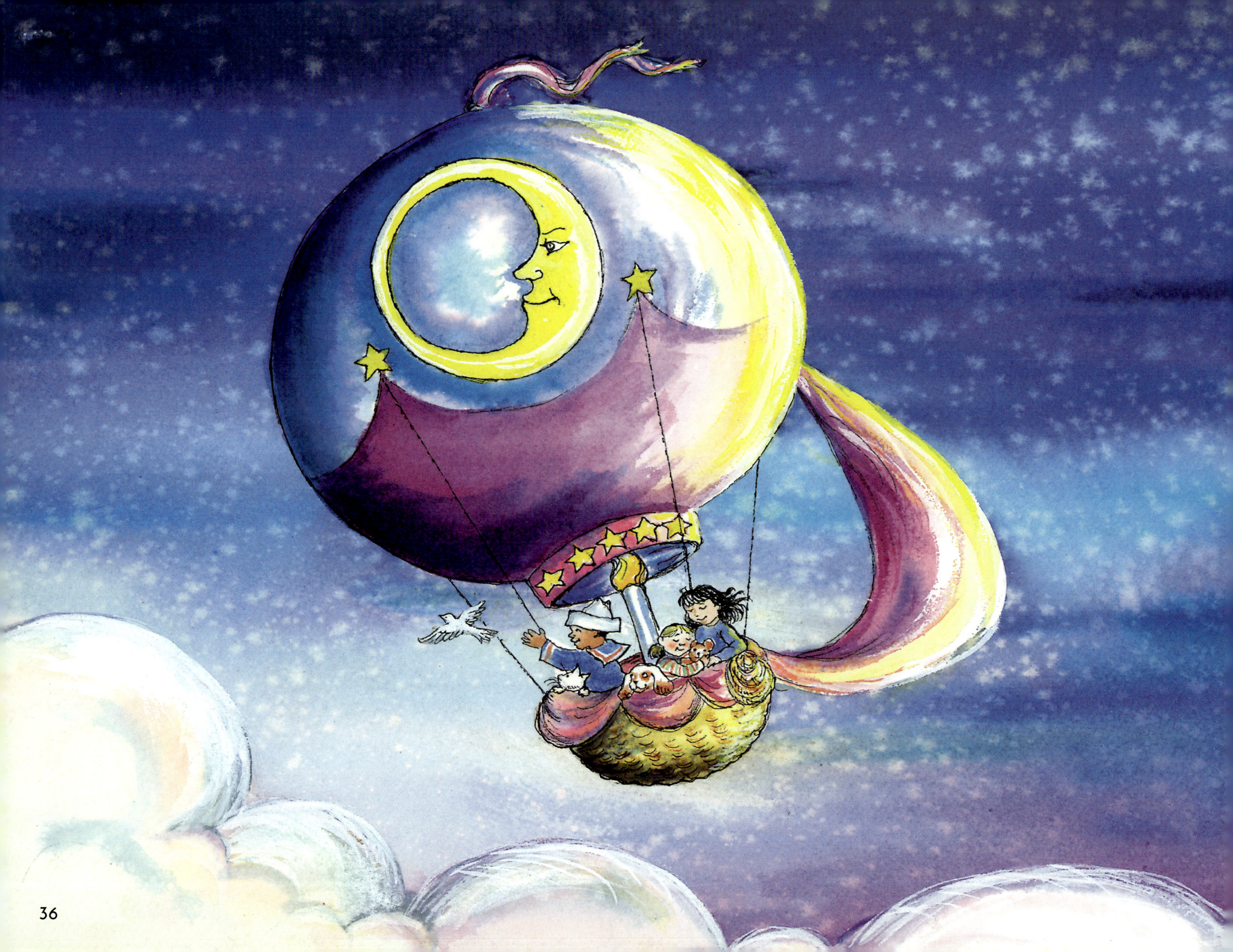

The Moon Balloon
will be here,
waiting to take you
on a journey.

Part II
When Images Speak Louder Than Words

Creating art has the power to help us find our way back to the soul – a journey of passion, exploration and healing.

J.D.

Your Companion for Inspiration

Creating images and symbols from my inner voice has been my mode of expression ever since I began drawing as a small child. I believe that creating art has the power to help us find our way back to the soul – a journey of passion, exploration and healing. Creating art, coming from our right brain, invites the imagination to open our hearts even during times of stress.

While working as Artist in Residence in a hospital pediatric oncology department, I found that the young patients often felt powerless, because everything was being done "to" them. They needed a safe and playful way to express their feelings – to be seen and to be heard. They needed a voice.

Their art became that voice, through a book, *The Moon Balloon*, which I created just for them.

I have witnessed how *The Moon Balloon* process has made a difference in the lives of hundreds of children and parents, both inside and outside the hospital. Now my observations have been validated by research showing how powerful the process really is.

I have discovered how important and beneficial this work is to all parents, children and caregivers, whatever your situation. A child does not have to be a hospital patient to benefit from using art for self-expression and healing. An adult using this book does not have to be an artist. The art will carry the message for everyone.

This process has strengthened me. It will strengthen you and open your heart to hope.

I am writing this book for you. This is your companion for inspiration.

Joan Drescher

Creating art invokes magic, both in the creator and in those who receive it. It makes the invisible visible.

J.D.

The Magician
Transformation

My Imagination Kart, filled with art supplies, covered with kites that spin and streamers that float in the breeze, catch the eye of six-year-old Arvin. He is receiving treatment in the Pediatric Oncology Outpatient Clinic at MGHC.

"I want to make a star wand just like that," he exclaims loudly, pointing to a star on the Kart.

For the next hour he creates a cardboard star, refusing all help from his elderly Indian grandfather, who accompanied him to the clinic that day. "I'm putting streamers at each point," he says to everyone in the clinic.

"Now I need a wand," he announces. As there are no "wands" in the cart I offer a red pipe cleaner. "That will not do," he exclaims, "I need a real wand." After much searching, the head nurse comes up with a rigid plastic tube to serve as the wand. When the star is finally attached he joyfully yells, "I have a magic wand!"

Pulling his "chemo pole" behind him he waves his wand over the head of each patient and shouts, "Make a wish!"

For that very moment all the worry and pain in the waiting room seems to be transformed by the power of a small boy who created art and believed in wishes. Months later, as he lay dying, too weak to create anything, his mother asked if I would come to his bedside and make some art just for him. Of course I would.

"Make a wish," I said.

"I wish I could be a magician and fly around doing magic."

I still see his small, frail body connected to beeping machines, cloaked in a makeshift cape, wearing a pointed hat, holding a paper star wand. His wish to do magic was granted as he ascended into another place, where God, healing and art are one.

Queen Aileen
Courage

I heard a familiar voice calling my name as I pushed the Imagination Kart down the corridor.

"Hey Joan," the voice said, "come into my room. I have something awesome to tell you." Aileen was a 12-year-old battling cancer of her leg. She had recently undergone seven surgeries. We had spent many afternoons creating art together while she received treatment.

As I entered her room, she ripped off her sheets, waving her newly amputated bandaged stump. "Say hello to Peggy," she said. "She wants to meet you. Remember how much pain I was in all the time? Well, it was my decision to have my leg amputated. They wanted to wait, but I believe there is more to life than just being in pain. I want to play softball again, and ride my bike. "I just want to live."

Handing me a painting of a crown she had made, she said, "They don't call me Queen Aileen for nothing. I am now cancer-free." I felt my heart expanding in the face of such courage and young wisdom.

Choosing to live takes courage.

J.D.

Uncovering Light Under Darkness
Hope

Saeed, a small frail boy of about six years with large black eyes, is so weak he can hardly speak. I don't know where his family lives; somewhere far away.

I put my head near his pillow to hear his thin voice.
"Would you like to do some art from the Kart?" I ask. He nods.

With the help of many pillows behind his back, he sits up to create stick figures representing his family from the other side of the Earth. We wrap the drawing paper around a plastic cup for him to keep - a treasure from his hospital experience.

Then I show him the scratchboard - stiff artboard covered with black that hides many colors revealed by scratching the surface.

He begins to scratch and his eyes widen. As the colors emerge, I feel his heart opening.

He becomes a magician, scratching away the darkness to reveal vivid colors, shapes dancing before him, bringing the board in his hands to life - a metaphor for his own existence.

"Can I keep them?" he asks in disbelief. "Yes, of course," I reply.
"They are your rainbows." A large smile covers his small face.

Hope is holding on to rainbows in the dark.

J.D.

The Pain-Free Hat
Freedom of Spirit

"If you focus on the stars
when you wear my hat
you will never feel the shot.
The pain disappears, just like that!"

Dorie, confined to her bed in Isolation, was awe-struck when I arrived in her room with the Imagination Kart.

Decorated with flowing streamers, moving kites and little bells, the Kart offered a kaleidoscope of enticing art materials. While I slipped out to get some water to paint with, the 12-year-old secretly borrowed all my Bingo Jars and painted her sheets.

Embarrassed by what she had just done, she covered her rainbow masterpiece with blue hospital pads.

"What will the nurses say?" she moaned.

"Designer sheets!" I exclaimed,
celebrating her outrageous spirit.

Our friendship cemented, our many art projects grew like a garden. Expressing her feelings about living with chronic illness, through sharing art and *The Moon Balloon* book, became a vehicle for Dorie and she wrote her own stories. One of her projects was to create a "pain-free hat" for kids to wear during difficult procedures.

She wrote a poem to go with it:
If you focus on the stars... The pain disappears just like that!

Her generous and creative spirit spilled over to the hospital community. Posted outside her door while in Isolation were Valentines for nurses, poems for doctors and art for other kids in the hospital.

Later, I was blessed to run into her while she was in Intensive Care, receiving treatment.
As a college student, and now as a graduate, Dorie thrilled me by telling how she passes the Moon Balloon process on to her friends who feel stressed, and shares her creative spirit to help others heal.

"Bonbolita"
Transforming Stress Through Beauty

Joanna, usually optimistic despite her battle with cancer, was clearly having a bad day. As I entered her room, the 14-year-old shared how angry she was to be back in the hospital again, this time with a fever, when she was planning to take part in the Run for Cancer.

"Just when I thought I was getting well, I'm sick again," she said, "and I hate the way I look without any hair. And they're talking about more chemo."

Together we explored the Stress Balloon, filling it with images of painful shots, blood being drawn, and beeping IV machines. After expressing, with vivid colors and images, the depressing feelings she was carrying around, she began to lighten up.

The next balloon she wanted to visit was the Butterfly Balloon. She wished to get better, and to be able to fly away like a butterfly. A nurse came into the room as she was drawing a beautiful butterfly. "'Bonbolita' is 'butterfly' in Portuguese," she said. "It is a symbol of beauty and transformation."

"Could I create a butterfly bouquet?" she asked. I found an empty glass vase and we began creating butterflies out of brightly colored tissue paper and pipe cleaners. We filled the vase with a bouquet of butterflies, which she held in her hands, and her brown eyes filled with tears. Her whole mood changed to one of joy. She became the very butterfly she was creating, a symbol of beauty and transformation.

The Blue Box

Gratitude

Large brown eyes; he is painting with intent, a jewelry box for his mom, who is working, while he lies in a hospital bed, alone, waiting for more surgery.

"She will really love this," he said, carefully brushing the paint all over the surface. "Blue is her favorite color."

The machines attached to his small body are humming. His tongue works around the corners of his mouth as he focuses on his task.
The box is filled with fear, separation, wanting, aloneness and love.

I see a tear roll down his beautiful face. "It's not perfect. I want it to be perfect for her. I messed up," he cries, holding the box in his blue painted hand. Two more tears roll down like mountain streams and slide off his brown round cheeks onto the box. I want to say to him, "You are the jewel in this blue box. Perfect in every way. Like you, it is filled with love and caring from your six-year-old soul. I hope your mom will keep it forever. It is a treasure." But, I say, "It is beautiful, just the way it is. Let it dry, and I'm sure your mother will love it. You did a good job."

I never meet his mom, but I want to say to her, "He cares so much for you. You, with all your burdens, working full time, other kids, being a single mom — he knows who you are. You are his hero. Just be there for him. Tell him that you see him, hear and love him, just the way he is. He is your perfect present. Be present. He is your jewel."

I am a child of the one light, a bridge between heaven and earth. When love flows across that bridge, miracles happen.

On Wings of Light

YOU MATTER

You've Got Mail
Unconditional Love

Delivering pieces of love, On folded paper

Like smiles and balloons, Opening a letter of love

Is like being thought of, All over again

Pointing at you, to you, Sitting with open arms

Undivided attention, For one moment in time,

Being seen as special. The mail comes

The heart opens

Liz Ennis

In my Kart
are white paper mailboxes for
kids to paint and decorate.
Tommy's eight-year-old eyes lit up when he saw them.

How do you tell your mom you're scared about painful shots when you're
supposed to be a brave eight-year-old boy and not a baby?
How do you say you're mad about the food restrictions, and just being in the hospital, when you'd rather be home playing with friends? How do you say you're really freaked out when your face swells up and you don't know what will happen to you next? How do you tell her all this, when you don't want to worry her?

Of course: the mailboxes!

First, get Mom to make a mailbox – so you do it together: yours and hers. Decorate your mailbox with bright blue paint. Draw airplanes on it. Make a flag from a purple rubber glove and a pipe cleaner.

Mom's is bright yellow. She puts flowers from the garden on it. It's beautiful.
When they are ready, you slip your letter in, and shout, "Hey Mom, You've Got Mail!"

How do you tell your son how much you love him, worry about him, and pray to God he will
come through the procedures all right, without being an overprotective mother? You write a letter.

Tell him you will always be there for him, whatever happens. Tell him how proud you are of him.
Let him know you don't have to fight the fight alone. You will do it together.
Fold the paper, apply a sticker, place it in his blue mailbox, raise the purple glove.

Message delivered: unconditional love.

Martin's Mandalas

Beauty and Joy

Martin, a delayed young non-verbal teen with limited control of his body, spent his hospital days in bed. He had a lot of time to himself. People found it hard to communicate with him and labeled him as depressed.

I introduced him to making huge colorful mandalas from oversized coffee filters. He was ambivalent about working with me at first, but as we worked he became more and more excited, which turned into joy. He wouldn't stop making them until we completely covered his hospital room — windows, walls and ceiling — with a riot of color. Soon, the nurses, seeing the mandalas from their station, came in one by one and acknowledged him for creating such beautiful art.

He began to feel that he was special, a feeling that was unusual for him. Soon, an audience of amazed and admiring nurses formed, watching Martin dance, arms flailing, feet pounding with delight in celebration of his creations, a gift of beauty to his caregivers.

Is this a blend of thought, color, and emotion whispering to the soul?

Or just the language of the heart, remembering beauty, when it is open?

Rejection

Finding Self Love

My own rejection was activated when I entered the room of 17-year-old Andy, who told me to please go away and take that darn *Moon Balloon* book out of his room. "It is kid's stuff," he said.

Some of the nurses in the hospital really wanted me to visit him, but they warned that I wouldn't get anywhere with him. He was there because of three failed suicide attempts. This time, I just brought art supplies, and demonstrated how he could express himself with colored chalk and watercolor. Watching him create, I sensed a sad and angry rage exploding within him. I left him some art supplies for the next day.

When I returned, I found his walls covered with paintings. They were amazing splashes of dark color and scribbles. We created together and stuck the art on the wall in his room.

"Now, I'm ready to read that stupid kid's book," he said, and grabbed it off my Kart. He drew a basket with disconnected strings, and on each side of the basket he drew red flames to represent the rage he felt.

It was easier for him to go into the Angry Balloon than into the Love Balloon. He said that he didn't love anyone and no one loved him, so why visit the Love Balloon. But I didn't give up. I asked him to create some art about what he loved and what he wished for. He began to cry, and said he wished he liked himself better, but there wasn't anything about himself that he liked.

After much coaxing and drawing, he shared that he liked taking care of animals, open spaces, fresh smells, and sunshine; he enjoyed building things; and he was a good carpenter. He felt he would like to help people, and that he had affected others in very small ways, by caring.

When I left, he told me how good this experience was for him, using art, and he said he would share the stupid book with others.

Dreamsweeper
When Images Transform

Bringing art into a hospital is not a fringe benefit. It becomes a doorway to the whole healing process. Art is a way of helping a child find internal control. It can help a child define their sense of competence and worth. My work is to connect with small souls; art is my offering, a surprise gift waiting to be opened. Blunt children's scissors with blue handles were such a gift for Samantha.

Samantha and I became friends after I introduced her to the art of cutting paper. I knew how angry the five-year-old was about living with a brain tumor. She began cutting the paper into smaller and smaller pieces until she had a huge pile on the playroom floor. Many of those watching her were afraid she would cut all her IV wires. But my giving her permission to cut was a major bond of trust for her to express all the anger she felt.

When Samantha had a recurring bad dream, and would wake up screaming, her mom asked if I would share *The Moon Balloon* book with her. I invited Samantha to go to the family room, a quiet place away from noise and all the other kids. Although she knew the book well, we read it all the way through together, and I told her she was in charge.

Normally, I visit one or two balloons with a child. She decided he wanted to visit all the balloons, and set her own pace.

When we went to the Dream Balloon, she drew the pictures right in the book, and began to tell me the story of her dream. As she spoke, I wrote the words to match her pictures.

Her dream was being in a car with a doctor. The doctor was driving very fast, and Samantha couldn't get out. She drew a chair, and said that she was strapped into it, holding on to the handles. I asked her how she felt being in the car, and she drew a picture of a scared face, with the mouth wide open, ready to scream. I asked her to describe everything in detail, and waited until she was finished before going to the next balloon.

The next balloon was the Angry Balloon. In it, she wrote "I'm mad because I have cancer!" and scribbled all over it. Although her parents were in the middle of a separation, she did not put them in the Angry Balloon.

When we went to the Tear Balloon, she said, "I am sad about always being in the hospital," and drew a hospital gown, "and always being attached to my IV," which she also drew.

She put her parents together in the Love Balloon, and ran down the hall with a big smile on her face, waving the book in her hand to share with her mom.

I know that *The Moon Balloon* helped her to communicate her beautiful creative spirit as a gift of love to both her mother and father. Later, we made a dreamsweeper, a cardboard moon that she cut out and painted and attached to the end of a wand. Every night before she went to sleep, she swept away all the bad dreams, until they disappeared completely. Shortly after our interaction, Samantha died. Through the gift of art and her own imagination, I believe she found peace, joy and a healing of her soul as she transitioned out of this life

Part III
Sharing Art Activities

Together we can make our dreams a reality.
J.D.

Being Present for a Child

Art is a universal language. Families from around the world experience the same emotions. Creating symbols and images can become a way of being seen, heard and understood, transcending language barriers. The sun, a universal symbol, touches people of all cultures and languages. Everyone can visualize its warmth. It seems to heal them with remembrances of a time when they felt in harmony. It is a wonderful way to engage a child in storytelling.

My work of bringing the arts to healthcare is also my indirect way of introducing wholeness through symbols. I have long used the mandala in murals for radiation rooms and cancer clinics. It represents wholeness and our connection to the infinite.

Using *The Moon Balloon* book engages a child in a safe and positive way. Although all artwork is copyrighted in my name, I give readers permission to photocopy the black-and-white pages for non-commercial uses only. In that way, those illustrations can be used for coloring again and again.

The Field of Balloons represents feelings. I usually begin a Moon Balloon journey by offering a positive balloon. The Star Balloon has a fish for a basket, and this is for making wishes. Every child has a wish.

Balloon images are containers for feelings. You can draw a simple oval shape to contain the wishes that you and the child will draw. You can learn a lot about a child by asking them what they wish for.

The Stress Balloon tries to help children identify and express their frustrations about things that are not working. Begin by sharing your own frustrations. You might point out that you can feel stress in your body. You could ask the child if they've ever had a stomach ache before a big test. Ask them to show you where they feel tension. Is it in the neck? In the shoulders or the back? Encourage them to draw a symbol of something that's not working. If the child can't think of something, you might give them an example, such as drawing an image of a clock to express your feelings of never having enough time.

Many children in my research drew examples of having too much homework, other kids that called them names, and not feeling "good enough." After a child has expressed their feelings in the Stress Balloon, you can visit the Peace Balloon. Here they can relax, and just be themselves.

You do not have to be an art therapist to know when a child would benefit from using art to express sad feelings. You might draw a Tear Balloon and ask the child, "What color is this balloon?" If the child you're working with is unable to speak about what is causing sadness, encourage them to just draw symbols that express feelings.

Parents often try to fix things. Some things just are, and we must just be with what is. They may feel helpless when a child has an incurable illness, but it is important to address everyone's feelings up front. Drawing and inviting the child to share is an important way to express the pain and sadness together. It offers the opportunity to learn more about what is really being felt.

Be prepared to hear sad stories about other situations, such as parents going through a divorce or losing a job, a fear of being bullied, or a pet who has died. When sadness is about loss, remind them that this is also a place to put memories and feelings that can be visited at a later time.

Let the child lead you as to how long you stay in this balloon. Ask if it's okay before going on to the next balloon. The Tear Balloon acknowledges the often overwhelming feelings and existence of sadness. Sometimes a child needs permission to be sad, without trying to hide it or be "strong" for the parent's sake. Let the child know that it's okay to cry.

My experience has been that children who are hospitalized often feel angry. School-age children are mad about not being able to go out to play or be with friends, and they miss being with family members. They are upset about having to get shots, take medicine and deal with pain, as well as the uncertainty that their illness presents.

You might begin by asking the child, "What color would anger be?", "What shape would it take?", "Does it have jagged lines?" You can help them identify their feelings by writing and drawing symbols, based on their responses. Some hospitalized children have expressed their anger by coloring paper black, tearing it up, or poking holes in it.

Encourage them to put their drawings into the Angry Balloon, which acts as a container. This allows the child to see and acknowledge their angry feelings, instead of carrying them in their bodies. This process will help you communicate with the child, whatever their age.

Sometimes teens feel embarrassed about sharing feelings. Many teens I approached during the research called *The Moon Balloon* "a kid's book." I often would leave the book with them for a few days, and come back to find that they had made many drawings and were ready to have a conversation. Sometimes I would engage them by drawing and asking them questions.

Let teens use the book in their own way, as a journal or a tool. Let them know there is no right or wrong way to express feelings.

Getting younger kids to express anger is easier than with teens. Don't be surprised if an older child kicks you out of their room. Teens often use the book on their own, and may share *The Moon Balloon* book with their peers.

I always end a session on a positive note. The Love Balloon provides closure after visiting some difficult emotions. Exploring the Love Balloon with a teen often becomes a way for them to discover self-love. Many teens are conflicted about themselves and their bodies. The goal is to experience giving and receiving love, and to learn kindness and empathy. No matter who the audience, these symbolic balloons help children and adults to communicate, opening hearts to healing.

Making Inspiration Soup

Begin with a large dose of presence.
Sprinkle with inspiration and curiosity and stir gently.
Add a little silly salt.
Warm the project with love until ideas begin to bubble.
Spice with bright color and imagination.
Share while it's still hot.

You Can Do It

- How does a mother who claims she can't draw a straight line introduce art to her child?
- How does a grandfather, with a strong commitment to helping his grandchild, enter the unfamiliar world of art?
- How can a nurse, whose day is filled with changing IVs and administering meds, take time for drawing and creating with a child?
- How can art possibly help a child who withdraws into a shell whenever adults come near to communicate?

Creating art with a child can be an essential part of healing from illness, trauma or the problems of everyday living. People who worry about having no art training need only recall their five-year-old self to help a child find the process of joyful creation. Simply be willing to explore and share the joy of discovery. Put down your cell phone and jump into this adventure. Creating trust, providing a safe space, and being present for them may be the best medicine you can offer.

Perhaps you might feel a bit anxious about introducing art to your child, as you don't think of yourself as a creative person. Don't be afraid, this is something you can do. Art is the bridge that will help you communicate with your child, whatever he or she is experiencing.

Children are blessed with creativity. We just have to get out of their way. When you share the joy of creating, you're opening the box of possibilities together. Just being present is your gift. You already have everything you need to do art with the child.

Creating art together is a way of discovering that your role is not to come and fix people or play hero(ine), but just to walk in their shoes. Together you can experiment and discover through different media. Be curious. Express feelings. Trust your own intuition. Whatever comes up is okay. Art is your friend.

Mandalas: Cathedral Windows

- Experiment with color
- Simple, quickly completed
- Joy of seeing a design unfold

Benefits
- Suitable for young child
- Offers more complex challenge for older child
- Suitable for child with limited mobility/disability
- Can be done together – child, parent, family
- Changes your environment

Supplies
- Coffee filters – 6" or 12" diameter
- Liquid watercolors or water-based dyes
- Bingo bottles – small plastic bottles with sponge tops
- Newspaper and tape

Fold coffee filter in half and again in thirds, like a pizza slice. Apply liquid colors to blend colors on the coffee filter. The colors bleed together and leak all the way through the layers creating a beautiful effect.
Open the filter, discover the pattern that has been created. Allow to dry. Display on a sunny window so the light streams through, creating the effect of a cathedral's stained glass windows.

Read "Martin's Mandalas," page 52

Cardboard Mandalas

- Simple and quickly completed
- Can be cut into many shapes
- Great for decorating IV poles

Benefits
- Humanizes technology
- Mixed media experience
- Durable
- Can be done together – child, parent, family

Supplies
- Pizza cardboards
- Tissue, ribbon
- Paints, crayons, colored markers
- Tape, glue, feathers, jewels, glitter, other found and fun materials
- One-hole punch

Just begin! Decorate the cardboard with any designs you like.
When ready, punch a hole in the edge of the mandala and thread the pipe cleaner through it to use as a hanger.

Scratchboard Art

- Immediate gratification
- Brilliant rainbow colors
- Transformation

Benefits
- For any age, child and adult
- Quick and easy
- Lends itself to great detail
- Perfect for someone with limited mobility

Supplies
- Scratchboard material with black ink that covers colored layers. Purchase from art supply store
- Wooden sticks, toothpicks or any common tool for scratching

Scratch away the dark layer and reveal brilliant colors below.
Experiment with different scratching tools.
Discover the designs hidden in the scratchboard.

Read "Uncovering Light Under Dark," page 45

The Pain-Free Hat

- Used in procedures that you know will be painful. Focus on the stars or items hanging down from the bill of the hat
- The child might think about and identify the source of their anger or pain
- An opportunity to bring inside feelings out

Benefits
- A way for the child to let others know that he/she is angry or in pain
- A way for children to use humor
- Appropriate for cancer patients and others with hair loss

Supplies
- Cotton baseball cap
- Magic markers, glitter, pipe cleaners, stars or charms
- White glue, fabric glue or glue sticks

Invite the child to wear the hat when they are angry, getting a shot, or in pain.
Can be used when feeling disappointed, for example, whendiscouraged about doing homework.
It is an expression of the child's feelings.
Change the decorations to fit what's going on.

Read "The Pain-Free Hat," page 46

The Mailbox

- Project for folks to exchange letters
- Creates ongoing interaction
- Lets people know that they are special

Benefits
- Getting a letter makes someone feel special
- A way of telling things that are hard to put into words

Supplies
- Paper mailbox found at Discount School Supply, or empty tissue box or shoebox
- Colored markers or tempera paints
- Paint brushes, construction paper, tissue, cloth or cardboard to make flag
- Pipe cleaners or popsicle stick for flag post
- Glue, tape, scissors, paper fasteners

Each person decorates a mailbox with things that are important to them, to make it their own. Use paint, magic markers, glitter, whatever you want.
Make a flag so you can raise it to let people know when there is mail inside.
Write a letter to someone you care about. Send a picture or a Valentine. When the flag is up, they know they've got mail. A great way to connect.

Read "You've Got Mail," page 50

A Treasure Box

- A container to hold precious things such as photos, letters, stones, jewels – treasures and things of fun and beauty

Benefits
- Allows revisiting places and things, and remembering people who are important to you

Supplies
- Paper box from Discount School Supply, or any box suitable for decorating. It can be small or large, old or new
- Colored markers or tempera paints
- Paint brushes, construction paper, tissue, cloth, ribbons, jewels, sequins, stuff you like
- Glue, tape, scissors

Decorate the box with your favorite colors and textures: paints, markers, cloth, paper, pictures. Add jewels, ribbons, sequins, anything that brings you joy.
Look for treasures everywhere.
Whatever reminds you of something is okay.
Put them in the box.
Visit it whenever you like.

Read "The Blue Box," page 49

The Magic Wand

- For making a wish, using the imagination
- Empowering people to make a difference
- Creating hope and dreams

Benefits
- Imagining and playing with what's possible and impossible

Supplies
- Cardboard or card stock to make a star shape
- Marker to trace the star shape, and scissors
- Wooden or plastic stick or tubing to make a wand
- Paint, ribbon for streamers, glitter
- Paint brushes, tape, glue

Have the child draw the star to make a pattern. Cut out the star. Decorate with glitter, streamers, and paint. Glue the star onto the wand. Have a conversation about how magic can be used. Ask the child to describe some wishes. Do a visualization about helping to bring good into the world by granting wishes for others. Think "Simple Acts of Kindness." Empower the child to use the wand's magic.

Read "The Magician," page 42, and "Dreamsweeper," page 54

Crown

- Confers courage
- Acknowledges special occasions
- Acknowledges the child as special

Benefits
- Especially appropriate for children going into surgery or through any difficult passage
- Celebrate any occasion from birthdays to losing a tooth

Supplies
- Cardboard or heavy paper to make a crown shape
- Marker to trace the crown shape, and scissors
- Paint, ribbon for streamers, glitter, jewels, stars
- Paint brushes
- Tape, glue, stapler, masking tape

Make a crown pattern on the cardboard and cut it out.
Fit the crown to the child's head.
Decorate with markers, glitter, jewels, stars, ribbons.
The child may wear the crown when they need courage.

Read "Queen Aileen," page 44

Free Drawing Murals

- Express emotions by drawing in the moment, whatever is coming up
- Draw without thinking or editing
- Draw with the whole body
- Choose colors that reflect where you are emotionally

Benefits

- Releasing emotions that you may not even know you have
- Takes one to a different place; often resolves stress/anxiety
- Observation of where you were and where you are

Supplies

- Bold colors: paint, oil crayons, colored markers, chalk
- Three large sheets of drawing paper, 11" x 14", 16" x 20" or larger

Express on the paper, WITHOUT JUDGMENT, drawing where you are right now, emotionally.
Use color and line to express strong emotions such as agitation, frustration, exhilaration. Notice where in your body you are feeling the emotions.
Draw a second time, noticing where you find yourself in a new moment.
Draw a third time, feeling your emotions yet again.
Look at your drawings and see what has changed.

Read "Rejection," page 53

Butterfly Bouquet

- Simple gift to yourself or others
- Transform feelings

Benefits

- Simple to make, simple materials
- The more you make, the more you share

Supplies

- Colored tissue papers – solids and patterns
- A sheet of heavy paper or cardboard
- Brightly colored pipe cleaners

Make a butterfly shape from heavy paper or cardboard.
Lay the pattern on tissues and cut several shapes from patterns and solids.
Assemble four tissues, alternating patterns and solid colors in layers.
Wrap a pipe cleaner around the center of the butterfly shapes, scrunching them together. Add more pipe cleaners to form the butterfly antennae, and a long stem to go into your vase.
Spread the wings to show all the colors.
Invite others to make butterflies with you.
Each friend and each butterfly is unique.

Read "Bonbolita," page 48

The Moon Balloon: Simple Drawing Techniques

- Trust your own creative abilities
- Draw simply, remembering your five-year-old self
- Let go of perfection
- Use your imagination
- Create a place for emotions that are too difficult for words

Benefits
- Creating a simple container in which to put feelings
- A way to open difficult conversations

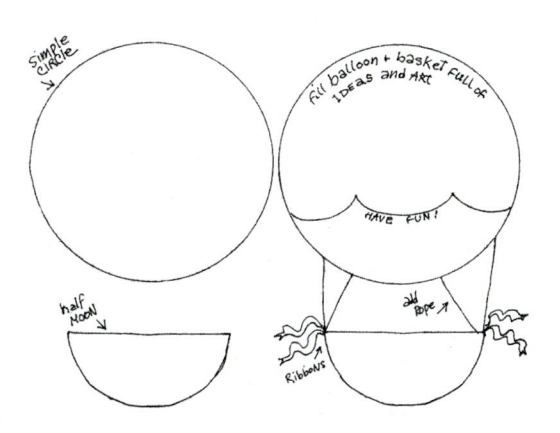

Supplies
- Large drawing pad
- Markers and chalk

Read or tell the story of *The Moon Balloon*. Invite children to express their feelings through drawings and symbols. Let children know that all feelings are okay. Everyone has them. Ask children to participate – let the child be in charge of the images. This is an interactive process between you and the child.

Read "Dreamsweeper," page 54

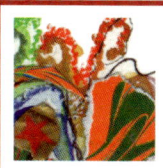

Supply List
What you need – Where to find it

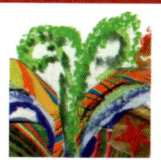

There are many sources of the materials needed for projects in this book. Below are the ones that I use most often, especially Discount School Supply, which has nearly everything I need, including odd items such as giant coffee filters, cotton baseball caps, and paper mailboxes. Pizza cardboards are available from School Specialty Products and from local restaurant supply companies.

Discount School Supply
www.discountschoolsupply.com

School Specialty Products
www.schoolspecialty.com

Michael's Stores Inc
www.michaels.com

Blick Art Materials
www.dickblick.com

Hobbycraft
www.hobbycraft.co.uk

The Works
www.theworks.co.uk

Your own home is a great source of art supplies as well, especially recycled materials that you might otherwise discard. Here are some ideas:

Gift boxes, shoe boxes, empty tissue boxes
Paper plates, coffee filters, food coloring
Gift wrapping paper and tissues, ribbon and string
Plastic bags, cellophane and plastic wrap
Vinyl and rubber gloves
Popsicle sticks
Used stamps
All kinds of brushes: Tooth brushes, make-up brushes, etc.
Feathers, shells, rocks, sticks, flowers, leaves

It almost goes without saying – craft and art supplies are readily available at your local Walmart, Staples, Dollar Stores, Target, and others. Your imagination is your only limit.

Part IV
Outreach and Resources

Art is the bridge to sharing joy, sadness and hope across the world.

The Moon Balloon Project

Art and Healing Around the World

The same sun, moon and stars shine down upon all people. These and other symbols found in the unique images in *The Moon Balloon* represent human emotions. The universality of these symbols and images embraces and impacts people wherever they are, whatever their language, whatever their heritage. People around the world find that the art and imagery of *The Moon Balloon* offer ways of communicating and expressing feelings when words are too difficult.

Thanks to the wonderful friendship of Dr. Tina Annoni and her husband, Mauro, *The Moon Balloon* has presented numerous cultural exchanges, workshops and trainings in Italy under the auspices of their nonprofit organization, Bluania. Among the institutions that have participated are the Gasolini Hospital for Children in Genoa and schools in Albissola and Varazze, and in the US, Massachusetts General Hospital for Children, and many Massachusetts elementary schools.

From Scotland to Sandy Hook: The Healing Continues

Within days of the 1996 publication of *The Moon Balloon*, a tragedy occurred in the small town of Dunblane, Scotland. Sixteen kindergarten children and their teacher were shot and killed. The Association for the Care of Children in Hospitals sent 725 *Moon Balloon* books overseas to help as a resource for coping with this unthinkable tragedy.

Dr. Harold Wilson, Principal Psychologist in Dunblane at the time, said, "This little book is one of the most helpful, and is rapidly becoming one of the most precious gifts we have received." Dr. Allison Russell, the new Director, is still using *The Moon Balloon* with families in Scotland.

The Moon Balloon brought its gifts to families who experienced losses in the World Trade Center tragedy of September 11, 2001, and it has been used around the world in Italy, France, Japan, Canada, Iceland, Holland, England, Scotland, the Philippines, and Alaska.

Today, this little book, like a phoenix rising from the ashes, is bringing its "precious gifts" to Newtown, Connecticut, to help that community heal from the tragic shootings at Sandy Hook Elementary School, where 20 first-graders and six adults were killed on December 14, 2012.

Dozens of families have received complimentary copies of the book from the town's Cyrenius H. Booth Library, under its "Books Heal Hearts" initiative.

Completing the Circle

Here in the US, the Moon Balloon process has been taught to caregivers in more than 100 hospitals, as well as pediatric hospices, and community volunteer programs. Over the years, The Moon Balloon Project has donated thousands of books to grief centers and other nonprofits that serve children experiencing trauma.

The language of images and symbols embraces communication, allowing a safe expression of feelings when words are difficult. *A Journey in The Moon Balloon: When Images Speak Louder Than Words* touches the lives of children, parents and caregivers alike.

The Moon Balloon Project, Inc, Building Healing Bridges for Children Through the Arts In Medicine, is a 501(c)3 nonprofit organization that inspires children to express their emotions honestly and openly through playful hot air balloon symbols. It provides a safe environment enabling children and families to communicate in stressful situations. Research on the Moon Balloon process at Massachusetts General Hospital for Children has shown that making art nourishes the spirit and helps the healing process of both body and mind in children. Our goals are to foster emotional literacy in all children, especially those who are ill, in transition, or experiencing loss, and to nurture creative connections between caregivers, educators, parents and children in America and around the world. We offer training and workshops for all those concerned with bringing emotional healing to children.

Learn more at www.TheMoonBalloonProject.org.

Recommended Resources

Organizations:
- Lesley University Institute for Arts in Health www.lesley.edu
- Mente Corpo Education/Bluania Onlus www.bluaniaonlus.org
- Joan Borysenko, Ph.D. www.joanborysenko.com
- Life is Good Playmakers/Project Joy content.lifeisgood.com/playmakers
- Child Life Council www.childlife.org
- Helping Children Cope Programs www.helpingchildrencope.org
- Colors In Motion www.colorsinmotion.com
- Spiritual Directors International www.sdiworld.org
- International Expressive Arts Therapy Association www.ieata.org
- Arts and Health Alliance www.artsandhealthalliance.org

Publications:
- *On Wings of Light, Finding Hope When the Heart Needs Healing*
  By Joan Borysenko and Joan Drescher www.joandrescher.com
- *Meeting Children's Psychosocial Needs Across the Health-Care Continuum*
  By Judy A. Rollins, Rosemary Bolig, Carmel C. Mahan
  www.rollinsandassoc.com/publications_books.html
- *The Little Magician*
  Curated by Sandra Bertman, Ph.D., FT, *Journal of Palliative Care*, Spring 2010
  sbertman@comcast.net
- *Arousing Curiosity: When Hospital Art Transcends*
  By Judy Rollins, Ph.D., *Health Environments Research & Design (HERD) Journal*
  Spring 2011   www.rollinsandassoc.com/PDFs/HERDRollins_final.pdf
- *The Journey Through Grief and Loss: Helping Yourself and Your Child When Grief is Shared*
  By Rob Zucker, MA, LCSW   www.robertzucker.com
- *The Art of Healing*
  By Bernie S. Siegel, MD www.berniesiegelmd.com/about/the-art-of-healing
- *Symbols of Hope and Healing; Using Art with Families and Children*
  By Joan Drescher and Liz Ennis   www.lesley.edu/journal-pedagogy-pluralism-practice/joan-drescher-liz-ennis/symbols-hope-healing
- *"To Embrace the Wholeness of Life" A Guiding Light for Joan Drescher*
  By Susan Bayley, *Anchor Magazine*, Fall 2014 www.stillharbor.org/anchor-magazine

Videos at www.themoonballoonproject.org/videos.html:
- *The Moon Balloon Song*
  By Ken Read-Brown, Pastor, The Old Ship Church, Hingham MA
- *Hingham Author Lifts Spirits With Children's Book*
  The Patriot Ledger, March 28, 2012
- *The Moon Balloon Donated to Newtown Library*
  News 12 Connecticut, January 12, 2013

The Moon Balloon Research

In 2010, Judy Rollins, Joan Drescher, and Mary Lou Kelleher completed research at Massachusetts General Hospital for Children that demonstrates the positive effects of images and symbols in helping children and families communicate with each other and cope with the stresses of hospitalization and illness. They also assist the medical staff to better serve their young patients. The stories in this book reflect the human side of the data collected in this research.

The article, "Exploring the ability of a drawing by proxy intervention to improve quality of life for hospitalized children," was published in *Arts & Health Journal*, February 2012.

www.rollinsandassoc.com/PDFs/ArtsHealth-MoonBalloon.pdf

Acknowledgements

Many friends, colleagues, and family members have helped me hold the vision of this book from the very beginning. I give heartfelt thanks to:

Susan Bayley, expert designer and loyal friend, with whom this book manifested through hard work, joy and laughter.

Anne Kimball, my friend and literary agent, whose vision for this book is to help children of our troubled world.

Reverend Suzanne Fageol, my spiritual director, who guided and supported me over the sometimes rocky road to completion.

Ken, my husband, and my children, Lisa, Kim and Kenny, who are a constant source of inspiration. I particularly thank Lisa, whose editing expertise is always available to Mom.

Jean Jacobs, my sister, with whom I share the journey.

The Moir Family, who continue to help and support The Moon Balloon Project, extending the vision of Ron Moir to reach parents and children in need.

The Moon Balloon Board, whose caring commitment continues to share this important work with others.

Joan Borysenko, my spiritual mentor and dear friend.

Judy Rollins, colleague, friend, and Moon Balloon supporter from the very beginning.

Liz Ennis, long-time friend and creative spirit.

Barbara Wollinsky, designer of *The Moon Balloon* book in all its stages of development.

Michael Melford and Dan Ciccariello for their legal guidance.

Esther Maschio, Deedee Sprecher, Barbara Sheehan, Anne Donnelly and Deanne Noiseux – supporters of creative works in process at the South Shore Art Center.

Tina and Mauro Annoni, Sandra Bertman, Linda DeHart, Nikki Hu, Mary Lou Kelleher, Susan Scherr, Vivien and Phillip Speiser, Susan Trausch, and Rob Zucker, friends who contributed in different and essential ways.

My dear forever friends Joanne Cavatorta, Elizabeth Torrey, and Syma.

Jane Bryant, my book dowser, and her husband, Cy.

Dr. Kate Angelo, my chiropractor, for keeping my mind and body together.

Reverend Ken Brown, for writing and performing "The Moon Balloon Song."

Bernie Siegel and Shaun McNiff for their long-time support.

Gratitude to everyone who had a role in the creation of this book – you know who you are.

About Joan Drescher

Joan Drescher has explored how art heals body, mind and spirit for more than 20 years. Her unique and colorful murals answer the need to humanize the healthcare environment and are found at major hospitals throughout the United States and Canada. As the recent Artist in Residence at Massachusetts General Hospital for Children in Boston, Joan has brought light and reassurance to the bedside of hundreds of hospitalized children and their families.

She is the director of the nonprofit, The Moon Balloon Project, Inc. which is dedicated to helping children and families to communicate and embrace the wholeness of life through images. See www.themoonballoonproject.org

Joan has trained a wide variety of professionals and clinicians in effective ways to use *The Moon Balloon* with children and families, even when they are feeling overwhelmed by their circumstances. She has worked with Child Life professionals, nurses, grief counselors, social workers, therapists, pediatric hospice workers, teachers, clergy, guidance counselors, and families to build a safe and supportive outlet to help children cope with the stresses of life-changing experiences.

She has authored and illustrated more than 25 books for children and adults, including *On Wings of Light*, with Dr. Joan Borysenko. Joan is a fellow at Lesley University's Institute for Body, Mind and Spirituality in Cambridge, Massachusetts. She is a Certified Spiritual Director from the Claritas Institute for Interspiritual Inquiry in Boulder, Colorado, and is a Gallery Artist at the South Shore Art Center in Cohasset, Massachusetts. Her prints and paintings can be seen at www.joandrescher.com

Photo by Ken Drescher

Author's Note

As an artist and a healer, my mission is to bring art and beauty into dark places. During times of illness and pain, we are often disconnected from the very source that connects us to Spirit, and makes us feel whole. Realizing that mission, I feel that any work of creativity evokes magic, both in the one who creates and in the one or many who receive.

Creating art and sharing it with others has taught me to trust the universe, follow my heart, and draw from the light within.

In today's stressful world, where trauma is an all-too-frequent occurrence, art is needed more than ever to help families around the world to heal. That is the mission of this new book: *A Journey in The Moon Balloon: When Images Speak Louder than Words*.

Beauty is the awakener that brings forth hope and wholeness. Art is the regenerative tool of beauty. Creating art has the power to help us find our way back to the soul.

While presenting workshops for children and caregivers around the world, I have found that the images in *The Moon Balloon* transcend all language barriers. The same emotions – anger, sadness, worry and joy – are understood through symbols, and friendship becomes our universal language.

The stories in this book bear witness to The Moon Balloon's work, and share its gifts. Here we have courageous stories of ordinary families and children, remarkable heroes opening hearts to hope, healing and connection to others. Each story is like a bright star, shining through the dark night sky.